Written by Dr. John Layke
Illustrated by Donald Benedict

PDIC and Puppy Dogs & Ice Cream are trademarks of
Puppy Dogs & Ice Cream, Inc.

For all inquiries, please contact us at:
info@puppysmiles.org

To see more of our books, visit us at:
www.PuppyDogsAndIceCream.com

This book is given with love...

To: _____

From: _____

Dr. John Layke

on Body Shaming

For a child on a playground subjected to a bully's torments, the emotional and psychological impact can be devastating. For decades, the media has portrayed beauty and desirable traits as something "good," while obesity and unattractive traits (larger noses, smaller chins, acne scars, balding) were often villainized – even in children's Disney movies. One's own perception of themselves can often clash with the harsh realities and cruel comments bestowed upon them during their childhood and adolescent years; some of which can extend well into their adult lives – altering their social habits, future goals, and dreams.

I was born into a simple and loving Catholic family in Milwaukee, Wisconsin, and I was taught from an early age to love and accept others as they are. The son of a school administrator, education was just as important as family was. It wasn't until I entered a new middle school in Eau Claire, Wisconsin, that I realized I was a scrawny, lanky kid surrounded by several larger classmates. Although I wasn't bullied, it was the first time I understood positive and negative physical traits. In the years to follow, I would attend college at Marquette University in Milwaukee, Wisconsin, work in Chicago for the then-named Anderson Consulting (now Accenture), move to Fort Lauderdale, Florida for medical school at Nova Southeastern University, return to Chicago for my general surgery residency at the University of Illinois Metropolitan Group Hospitals, and eventually complete my training in Long Island, New York in plastic surgery residency. I saw people from every size, shape, ethnicity and background, and I learned ways to assimilate into each group, and to accept and relate with each person I encountered.

As a Beverly Hills plastic surgeon, I have not only trained to "beautify" and "youthify" individuals, but I understand the thought processes that go into why people desire certain traits. According to several research studies, people who are considered physically attractive are more likely to be interviewed for jobs and hired, they are more likely to be promoted in their careers, and they earn higher wages than those considered conventionally "unattractive." In addition, declining self-esteem is directly related to mental health illnesses like depression and anxiety. Now, I am not working myself out of a career, as plastic and reconstructive surgery will always play a role in society; but I do think that many newer trends stemming from social media are unhealthy and contribute to many mental health issues and social stigmas.

This dogmatic belief that "beauty breeds happiness" needs to be shifted in a positive, mutually responsive, and productive way. This book graciously starts the process early, simplifying the importance of being unique. It allows our children to understand at an early age that they will encounter other kids with different shapes, characteristics, or handicaps and that every single one should be viewed as special. As a father of three toddlers, it is my hope that this book allows me to connect with them and impress upon them the concepts of love and acceptance... And that other families are able to take this book – and lesson – to heart as well!

No body is the same,
And each is beautiful to see.
We are all wonderfully unique,
Even you and me!

Here are some of our friends,
Who look different in a way,
But all with hearts of gold,
Who live with joy each day.

Selma is a girl who's tall,
And can reach up really high.
She can pick the biggest apples,
And pretends to touch the sky.

Brandon is a boy who's small,
And likes to hunt for bugs.
He can crawl into tiny spaces,
Like no one else can or does.

Marigold is a girl who's skinny,
With beautiful light brown skin.
She dresses as a superhero,
And the villains never win!

Jenny is a girl who's big,
Who loves to boogie and dance.
She pirouettes for the crowds,
As they clap with each twirl and prance.

Michael is a boy in a wheelchair,
Who loves rolling through the town.
He plays basketball with his friends,
And scores the most points all around.

Sam is a girl with red hair,
That's vibrant, curly and poofy.
It goes every which way you can think,
And feels both springy and floofy!

Ronnie is a boy with glasses,
That are always on his face.
But when he swings a bat,
His team always gets first place!

Angela is a girl with freckles,
Like polka dots on her skin.
They jiggle whenever she giggles,
And run from nose to chin.

Everyone is special,
Different in their own way.
But sometimes bullies tease,
Being mean with what they say.

They may poke fun of your belly,
Your clothing, or your feet.
They can make you feel sad,
Or heartbroken with defeat.

...But those people don't matter,
So pay them no mind.
Show them patience and peace,
It's always better to be kind.

If kindness doesn't work,
Please don't take it to heart.
Find an adult to help,
They're usually quite smart.

Some of these big bullies,
Have their own set of troubles.
They feel bad about themselves,
And burst other people's bubbles.

Because we should all feel special,
Like beautiful works of art,
Having different bodies,
Is what sets us all apart.

Imagine just how silly,
If we looked exactly the same.
Wouldn't that be boring,
And also incredibly lame?

Being different is awesome,
From our heads down to our toes.

So, no matter what we look like,
Freckled, chubby or small,
All sorts of different colors,
Skinny, disabled, or tall...
Loving the body we have
Is the most important feature of all!

Claim your FREE Gift!

 Visit:

PDICBooks.com/Gift

Thank you for purchasing

No Body is the Same

and welcome to the Puppy Dogs & Ice Cream family.
We're certain you're going to love the little gift
we've prepared for you at the website above.

CPSIA information can be obtained
at www.ICGtesting.com
Printed in the USA
LVHW071929070723
751697LV00002B/11

9781957922355